A Crack
in the
Foundation

By C.M. Guidroz

Warning:

This book contains scenes and subject matter

that are graphic, disgusting, horrifying, bloody,

disturbing, and downright wrong. If blood, poop,

boneless children, violence, SA, domestic violence,

genital mutilation, suicidal thoughts, or vomit is a trigger

for you, please DO NOT READ THIS BOOK. This is a

story that is meant to cause an emotional reaction,

meaning I wrote this with the intention of disgusting

you, making you angry, making you wonder how this

could possibly be allowed to be published, and making you uncomfortable.

You may ask yourself, how can this be allowed to be published? But I follow up with a more important question, Why are you reading it? You can turn back now and never read what's beyond this page. No one needs to know. I won't tell. But if you decide to go forward, don't say I didn't warn you.

Prologue

The smell hits me before I can reach the front door's threshold. Anyone who does my line of work can recognize this smell. Some say it has a sweet aroma to it, but I disagree. The putrid, sour smell will cut your breath; no matter how hard to try, you can never get it out of your nose or memory. The smell of rotten flesh will haunt you forever.

"Nixon, we're down here," Paul calls to me from behind the stairs. Paul and I have worked together for over ten years; I've never seen him this upset. Pausing at the top of the stairs leading into the basement, I know it has to be bad to have Paul this anxious, and the smell feels like it wants to knock me off my feet from where I stand. My attempt to cover my nose doesn't help as I take each step down into the dark basement.

"I have never seen something like this in all my life. This is the kind of shit you only see in movies. I just don't.." Paul's sentence ends abruptly when he gags on his words. My eyes slowly trail from the blood splatters on the ceiling to the mass of bodies and gore laid out in front of me on the floor. My mind instantly tries to reach some sort of rational explanation for this scene, trying to make some excuse for the mayhem before my eyes. Did a wild animal get to these poor people? There is no way a human could have done this. Right?

Chapter One

The bed moves, the springs making a sound so shrill that the pounding in my head is amplified enough to wake me up. Looking over, blinking several times to try to clear the haze in my eyes, I see a woman I don't recognize stumbling to the bathroom. "What the fuck, man." I groan, reaching over. I tilt and shake each beer can, trying to find one with a sip left in it. Finally, my hand finds one, and I bring it to my lips, allowing the lukewarm beer to coat my dry tongue. When I feel like my head won't explode, I attempt to sit up in bed, I can hear whoever the woman was retching and the vomit splattering the toilet bowl from where I sit. In my hungover stupor, I look around and try to piece together the events that lead me here. I'm naked, and judging by the sour smell and dry flakey brown shit surrounding the head of my dick, I would assume I had a pretty eventful night.

The door to the bathroom opens, and I immediately recognize the mystery woman. Mikki is one of my regulars, I slide her a little cash, and she lets me do all kinds of nasty shit to her. I don't really like her, but I'm nice to her, and I think she likes me. I don't slap her around like a lot of these other men around here do, and I think that's why she lets me get away with only giving her a few dollars. She lays back in bed, the sounds of the springs attacking my headache once again. I look over and see the vomit still clinging to the strands of her hair. She's not an ugly woman, just one of the few women that lost their way around here. She got hooked on the wrong shit and linked up with the wrong people. I wonder what she was like before she was this shell of a woman.

"You really did a number on my ass last night, Slick; I'm sore." She complains. I rub my face, trying to find the energy I need for the day.

"I'm sorry. I got a little carried away, I guess. You got your money?" I ask without looking at her. I don't want her to think I want any more from her; I need to clean the crust off my dick and get out on the street if I want to make enough money today for my own vices.

"Yeah, I think so." She says as she gets up slowly to start looking for her clothes. One thing about Mikki is that she can take a hint. She knows the routine. I wait for her to get dressed, partly because it's the nice thing to do after I tore her ass up last night, but mostly because I don't trust her not to steal anything. I don't have much, but what I do have, I want to keep.

She grabs her things, and I stand to see her out the bedroom door. Before leaving, she turns around and pecks me on the cheek, the pungent smell of vomit still heavy on her breath. "See you later, Slick." She says as I watch her walk through the living room, rattling empty cans and crossing over piles of leftover shit my roommates left out. Once she is out the door, I feel comfortable enough to hit the shower. The water isn't nearly as hot as I want, but I've learned to take what I can get. After cleaning off the remnants of the night before, I get dressed and ready for the day. I don't mind that my clothes smell or that my face hasn't seen a razor in weeks because my job doesn't require me to look presentable. I'm a self-proclaimed professional panhandler.

I pay my share of the rent by standing on the streets and looking the way I do. I feed off of people's need to feel like they did something good for the day. Somehow, giving me a dollar or two will absolve them of all the other shitty things they did that day. Sure, I'm taking from homeless people by doing this, but I had to learn at an early age that this really is a dog-eat-dog world. Every man for himself or you don't survive. I didn't make them homeless; this fucked up economy and the rich assholes that run this country did. So why should I feel bad for trying to get my piece of this fucked up shit pie that is life?

Stepping into the living room, I see that my roommates, Kip and Josh, had pizza last night. The open box is lying on a passed-out Kip's lap. I grab a slice without waking him and proceed to find my keys. Yes, I have a car; how else would I get to all my usual spots across town? I'm careful to park far away from the place on the sidewalk I will be posted up; I don't want to be exposed on Facebook. People love to try and expose you for the piece of shit you are. I thought social media was supposed to make everything shitty look better; you know, your life sucks but pose for this selfie. I don't understand it; just another way for people to not mind their own fucking business.

After finding my keys, I make the short trip to my first stop. I usually make most of my money on this street. The street is full of corporate assholes, but it's not too upscale to where they run off anyone begging for money. A bonus is that I get to see her, I don't even know her name, and she's never even noticed me. She just smells so fucking good. I know that sounds weird, so let me explain; I saw her twice last week. She's tall, blonde, and so clean. She must work around here, but I've never been brave enough to follow her. She is always preoccupied with her phone when she passes me. One day she stopped to grab a pretzel from the loudmouth asshole that sells them not far from me. I hate that guy. I decided then to take two dollars from the money I made that day and buy a single salted pretzel. Nothing too crazy, just a homeless man using what little money he collected to buy the scrap of food that is a pretzel. I was able to stand behind her, and her sweet scent attacked my senses above all the other smells surrounding us. I leaned closer, trying not to be too obvious; I'd never experienced a woman that smelled like this. I know it's perfume, but it mixes with her musk, instantly making me want to bottle it up and inhale it while I beat my dick.

This is the type of woman that would never see the likes of my bed. I would be too embarrassed even to bring her home. No, this woman is like a painting in one of those fancy museums. You can look all you want but keep your fucking hands off; you'll only ruin her. She bought her pretzel and left me standing there in a haze, drunk off her smell.

Until that stupid prick yelled at me, "Hey, I don't give handouts. Take your high ass down the street." He barks at me.

"Fuck you, you sell stale ass pretzels on the street. You're no better than me." I yelled back, leaving without buying a damn thing because fuck him.

Now, every day I look forward to the off chance I may see her pass again. I just want to smell her. God, I sound like a fucking freak. Maybe I am, but it's something about her. She always looks so stern and serious; she's probably a real bitch. If only I could bottle up her scent, I'd spray it on Mikki before I plug all her holes again. I could close my eyes and pretend it was her taking my dirty dick. I laugh to myself and push down the semi-erection I have. No one will give a dime to a man begging for money with his dick saluting everyone.

People pass me by dropping dollar bills and change in the small cardboard box I set up in front of me. I mentally count what I have; once I reach an amount I'm ok with, I get up and move to the next location across town. Today I don't need to make much; I have most of my share of the rent saved up. I just need to make seventy dollars today, enough to finish my share of the rent and more than enough to buy me a few cases of beer. I like to consider myself a simple man; I chose one vice, alcohol. I've tried the other shit a few times, but it's not my thing. I'll take a bump here

and there if the occasion is right, but mostly, I just drink
until I pass out.

    I'm about to pack things up when I see her.
She's on the phone, of course, but it's her. She passes
me, then does something unexpected; she stops and
grabs the change out of her purse and drops it in my
box. I don't look up at her because I'm embarrassed
now that she's noticed me. She never stops talking on
the phone; she drops the change and keeps moving.
Her dropping the coins felt more like she didn't want the
loose change instead of her trying to do something
nice. There was something endearing about that; she
didn't give me the sad look everyone else does. She
didn't try to fake sympathy. I don't know what primal
urge comes over me, but I wait a moment, never really
losing sight of her, and I get my things. My body has
made the decision to follow her today before my brain
can comprehend what the fuck I'm doing. No one
notices me following her because most people try their
best to avoid making eye contact when they see me.
They don't want to give me anything, so they try to
make it seem like I don't exist. Which is working in my
favor as I watch her wait and cross the street. She

walks into an office building about a block away from my usual spot. This whole time she has been right there. I feel something shift in me standing on that street corner. I feel a sense of entitlement like I deserve something good in this fucking shit world.

I decided right then and there that I was going to follow her. Following her won't hurt anyone; I mean, sure, it's considered stalking to some people, but it's all about perspective. A lot of things in life are all about perspective. I won't hurt her; hell, I won't even talk to her. I just want to know her while remaining the background character in her story. That's all.

Chapter Two

The salty dough burns my tongue for a moment as I chew the pretzel I stole off the asshole cart today. He wasn't paying attention, so I swiped one off the little rack; once he realized, I took off running, flipping him the finger as I made my getaway. I won't be back on that street anyway. You can only stay in one spot for so long. I take another bite and sit back in the seat of my dark car. I'm parked in the spot I have claimed for myself a few houses down from my mystery woman. Well, she's not so much of a mystery since I've been stalking her for a little over a week now.

I was able to overhear her name when he husband called out to her from the driveway; Shelli is her name. She looked more like Ashley, in my opinion, but I don't know shit. I figured she would be married, even though she looked like the strong independent type. I only watch her when she's at home; I never follow her. I've wanted to, but every time she gets in her car to leave, I get nervous pulling out of the security of my parking spot. I don't want my cover to be blown. I like watching her at home because these are the kinds of people that leave their curtains open. I didn't know people did that in real life. They act as if no one can see them. Unfortunately, they only leave the curtains downstairs open; I've never gotten one of those nice undressing views like in the movies. Which is probably good since I would be the weirdo found beating his dick in a parked car.

They don't seem to be affectionate with each other. The husband seems like he's a "yes-man." He is a real pushover in a pair of dockers; I can tell from the way she bosses him around. She points, and he moves; I knew she was probably a real bitch. Who knows, maybe he's into that kind of thing. Some men like for women to call them pathetic and make them bark like a dog. I tried it once, but it wasn't my thing. The front door opens, and there she is in a tight black dress that hugs her body. I sink lower in the seat even though they never notice me. I'm always the person in the background; I play the part well. The truth is probably that people are so wrapped up in their own self-centered lives that they never notice when someone like me is parked outside their home for a fucking week.

"Just grab the card; we are going to be late." She barks as she shakes her head, walking to the big black SUV parked in the driveway. I wish I could roll down my window, hoping to catch just one lingering hint of her smell in the wind. If only I could find a way to bottle her scent, I wouldn't be parked out here every other night. I've made peace with the fact that I'll never be with a woman like her, and I wouldn't want to. The amount of pressure I would be under to perform to her liking is enough to make my dick turn in on itself. No, I would dirty her up and ruin the scent. Especially since the last few times I dipped my dick in Mikki, I've had a wicked itch and a putrid, yeasty smell every time I piss. Mikki doesn't seem to mind; she just wipes the thick yellow smegma from the corners of her mouth and keeps it moving. She's a professional, that one.

Captain Dickhead finally leaves the house, holding the white envelope up to show her. I can see her shake her head from the car, showing how unimpressed she is with him following her directions. Shit, if this rich prick can't make her happy, I sure as hell never would. He traded in his dockers for a suit tonight; they must be going to some fancy event. Which means they will be out of the house for a few hours at best. I shake my head, dismissing the thought before it can enter my head. "Slick, don't you even fucking think about it." I scold myself, my voice filling the empty car.

I haven't broken into a house since I was a teenager, but I remember it being easy. I know for a fact they don't have an alarm system because they never stop to set anything when they come in or out of the house. I could get in, grab her perfume and a pair of panties, and I'd be set. I could hold them up to my nose as I drilled Mikki, imagining that this pretty pussy finally gave a man like me a chance. My head tilts back, and my eyes close as I pretend to inhale that sweet scent; my hips start to thrust in the seat, my dick pushing at the steering wheel.

"Fuck, man, stop," I come out of my thoughts abruptly. Who the fuck am I? Obsessed with the smell of a woman like some pathetic freak. They backed out of the driveway and headed down the road, but my heart was racing. I could be in and out before they return; I won't take anything they would notice. I could do this. I stare at the house, mentally walking to the front door, getting into the house, and making quick work of it. Panties and perfume, that's it.

"Slick, what the fuck is wrong with you, man?" I ask myself. I wait another ten minutes in case they may have forgotten something and need to come back. When there is no sign of them, my body does that thing where it betrays me, and I'm out of my car, making my way up the sidewalk in front of their house. Fuck, I'm really going to do this.

Chapter Three

My heart is beating like a set of drums in my ears, but my body is determined to get its fix. I'm on the sidewalk, looking left and right for any signs of life. I've been parked on this street for over a week, and no one has batted a fucking eye. People come and go in their own little worlds, never noticing me; good thing I'm just an obsessed freak instead of a serial killer. I could be a ruthless murderer, canvassing the neighborhood for his next kill. They make it so easy to be watched, always on their phones or rushing to get their to-do list done. No one else matters in their world; they are the oblivious deer dipping their heads in the water, not knowing it's filled with crocodiles waiting to tear it apart.

I'm no crocodile, though; I'm just a sick freak obsessed with a smell. Like a hound dog latched on to the scent, I'm harmless. I've never hurt anyone in my life except for that asshole Kurt in middle school who tried to make me eat dog shit. He had it coming, bullying me every day. My dad saw my lip busted one day; when he asked how it happened, he gave me a black eye to match for being such a pussy. I knew I had to stand up to him, so one day after school, I gave Toddy, one of the older kids, four cigarettes and a random pill I found out of my daddy's stash to beat up Kurt for me. I stood there watching as Kurt's head bounced off the pavement with each punch, wincing every time. I guess I really was a pussy. Kurt never fucked with me again, giving Daddy one less reason to smack me around.

I don't look around too long; I don't want to seem suspicious. I make my way up the porch like I own the place. I slide out a random card from my wallet; looking down, I realize it's from the pet store in town. I don't have a pet; I can barely care for myself. The card is from when I was set up on the east side of town panhandling, and this dog would stay around. I felt like I was intruding on his corner, the way he would stay back and watch me. I would call out to him, but he would never come to me, just watch me from afar. I guess a lot of people were mean to him; I've always had a soft spot for animals, though. Finally, one day, I had a decent amount of money, and I decided to go into the pet store in town and buy a small bag of food. The next day I went out to do my normal day's work and dumped a pile of dog food a few feet away from me. He took his time getting closer and closer until one day, the hunger was enough to make him say fuck it, and he came up and ate from the pile. We all throw danger to the wind sometimes when it comes to hunger and urges; there is a small line that holds us back until we say fuck it. I guess that's what's happening right now. The line I wasn't willing to cross is no longer there because the hunger is too intense. Also, in my mind, I have played it out so well. I've made it seem too easy not to take advantage of. I will be in and out, and no one will notice I was here.

I slide the card back and forth in the door, panicking when it doesn't give immediately. I feel like a dozen eyes are on me, watching me break into this house, even though I know there aren't. I look around again to make sure; my hands are sweaty and starting to shake. I haven't done this shit in years; I remember it being way easier. Finally, I feel the door give and open. I look around again to ensure no one is watching, then slip into the house, closing the door behind me. The house is huge, just the foyer is bigger than my kitchen. I'd swear no one even lived here if I didn't know any better. Everything in this massive house looks so clean and polished. The staircase is the first thing you see; it has one of those handrails that you want to slide down. Turning to look out the window, I barely touch the curtains. I feel like one giant dirty fingerprint just standing in this house. My heart sinks for a moment when an SUV's headlights are slowly coming down the road. They wouldn't be back already, right? Fuck. What am I doing here? I move out of the window, my chest tight while I wait for the headlights to brighten the window, letting me know I'm caught. When I don't see any lights, I risk looking out the window, seeing the car's tail lights pass the house—false alarm.

"Get what you want and get the fuck out of here," I tell myself. I can't help but want to look around. You can tell a lot about a person by how they keep their house. In my case, I'm a dirty scumbag, so my place reflects that. This woman is just as clean as I thought she was, everything polished and looking brand new. I fight the urge to look around downstairs because I know what I want is up those stairs. Taking them one by one, the stairs groan under my feet. In the house's silence, they seem louder than they are, like they are trying to alarm anyone that an intruder is in the place. Opening the first door, I come to, I look inside, seeing it's just an office, not what I'm here for. I stand in the hall and sniff the air as if I could somehow smell my way to what I'm looking for. The air smells cool and fresh, not giving away the location of what brought me this far into my delusion. You would think I have always been obsessed with smells, but I can assure you I have not. Hell, even Mikki's can of sardines she calls a pussy doesn't turn me off from getting what I want. I don't know what it is about this woman's scent, but I've come this far, and I'm not leaving without it.

As I open the next door, I know I've hit my mark; the made-up bed full of fancy pillows is the first thing I see. Stepping in, I picture Shelli lying out waiting for me, naked with her fingers already deep inside herself. "Honey, I'm home," I smile, rubbing the hard-on that's already pushing against my zipper. My eyes land on the open door to the right that leads into the bathroom. Rubbing my hands together, I smile and walk across the polished wood floor, knowing I will find what I need in this room.

Flipping on the switch, I squint my eyes at the bright lights of the bathroom. "This is insane," I laugh to myself because the size of this bathroom is ridiculous. I've never seen a bathroom this big before in my life. I don't have much to compare it to, but having a bathroom this size is not normal. The door between the giant tub and the even bigger shower is a mystery to me, but I open it. The air hits me, and all I can do is smile; this is it. I inhale deeply, taking in the smell that brought me here. Clothes line the walls, all hung together by color, and a wall of shoes stacked neatly sits on the left. In the middle of the room is a vanity lined with fancy bottles. I take each one in my hand, lifting them to my nose, looking for the scent that has driven me mad for weeks. I start to lose hope, and my nose starts to burn as I place the third bottle down. Only one bottle is left, a dark bottle that looks almost black. I lift it to my nose, and I'm hit with the aroma that has mesmerized me enough to bring me here. "There you are," I say to the black bottle in my hands; even the bottle looks like some dark magic potion. A potion used to put poor helpless men like me under a spell, a spell that makes a man do crazy things, like break into a house.

Now, I only need a pair of panties, and I can get out of here. Feeling my dick still raging against my zipper, I make a mental note to rub one out in the car so I don't have to drive myself crazy with the smell the whole way home. I open drawer after drawer, looking for the perfect pair of panties, when my eyes land on the small clothes hamper near the door. Flipping it over and dumping its contents on the floor, I see exactly what I need. As if the gods of filth have looked down upon me, a pair of black used panties stares back at me from the floor. I pick it up and crumble it in my hands; the soft material feels nice and expensive. I open the fabric to see the exact spot where her pussy meets the fabric, and my eyes go wide. A small patch of something dry and white is in the middle of the fabric. I breathe in the material, and my eyes roll back in my head at the primal urges this scent brings out in me. A musk is so sweet with subtle hints of sweat; I run my tongue across the spot, hoping to get a taste of her.

At this moment, I know what has me so feral for this woman. She is the embodiment of what my life could have been. I could have been successful if I wasn't dealt the shitty cards I was dealt. I could have had a woman like this and not feel like just me touching her would ruin her. I'm cursed; my whole bloodline is cursed. We all fall into the same cycle of giving in to our vices. Our weakness turns into aggression, and we ruin everything we touch. They say to break the cycle, but I've spent more time than I can count trying to figure out how to do that, and it only drove me deeper into debt and deeper into the bottle. This woman's scent reminds me of what my life could have been. I can't have her, but I will take this with me, and maybe if I can pretend enough, it will manifest me out of this bullshit life I've been given.

Isn't that how all that manifestation shit works? You believe you have it, and you will have it. I'll close my eyes, inhale her scent, and imagine I'm fucking her raw in our mansion. I'll have her screaming, "Oh Slick, I can't believe I wasted my time with that dickhead of a husband when I could have had you. You fuck me better, Slick." As she meets each thrust I give her.

My balls ache just thinking about it, and as I walk out of the closet, I have to stop and look at myself in the mirror. My eyes are heavy-lidded with a caged lust I could barely contain. I won't make it to the car; I need to ease some pressure. The sound of my zipper is loud in the silent bathroom as I take my sweaty dick out and into my hand. Spitting in my hand, I run it up and down my stained cock as I grip the panties in the other hand. I wince slightly as my hand rubs roughly against the open sore at the head of my dick. I try not to think about the fact that it hasn't gone away in over a week, and I keep having to peel my boxers off of it from the leaking pus. Re-adjusting my hand to avoid it better, I start to get a good rhythm and have to brace myself against the counter. I hold the panties up to my nose and inhale deeply, her hypnotic scent forcing my balls to tighten, and I know I'm about to nut.

I look around for something to cum in; I don't want to ruin the panties with my own juices. My eyes land on a bottle of mouthwash, and I smile to myself. It looks expensive in a dark green bottle, not like those clear ones. I could shoot my nut in there and relish in the thought that she would be swishing my jizz around in her mouth. The thought has me scrambling to get the top off just in time to see my thick, yellow cum oozing into the bottle. My body feels like it's been electrocuted, feeling my toes tingle with the sensation. I make sure to get every last drop in the bottle as I squeeze the head of my dick, the rest of my thick cum mixed with a slight tinge of blood from that sore slides down the bottle.

"Fuck, that was intense." My voice echoes off the walls. I shake it off and slide my dick back into my pants. Putting the panties and fancy perfume bottle in my pocket, I quickly look around to ensure I didn't leave anything out of place. I've lost track of time in here, and I should probably get going now that I've got what I came for. She will probably think she misplaced the perfume; I mean, who breaks into a house and only steals perfume? She won't think someone else has been in here. One more look over, and I'm making my way down the stairs. My foot reaches the last step as the headlights flood the glass on the front door. Rushing to the window, I carefully peek out to see the SUV parking in the driveway. They are home, and I am still in the house. How the fuck could I have been so stupid?

I was thinking, with my fucking dick, that's what. I could have been out of here before they arrived if I didn't have to rub one out. I'm fucking weak, and now I'm caught. My body makes panic circles as I look for a place to hide, my heart beating in my ears. I hear them talking as they make their way to the front door. I rush behind the staircase, bracing my back against the door behind it. This must be the basement. The lock clicks and my heart sinks as they enter the door. I'm trapped like a rat, and it's only a matter of time before they find me.

Chapter Four

"I'm exhausted. I wish you wouldn't have invited Hanson over." I hear her say, and I'm trying to slow my breathing. The voice of the woman that got me into this damn situation fills the room. Why she had to go and put me under her spell? Shaking my head, I feel so stupid. My body jumps at the sound of two thumps on the floor. She must have taken off her heels. The sound echoed through my bones. I'm hyperaware of every single sound as I try to place their location in the house so I can sneak the fuck out of there.

"Why not? I mean, this is the foundation of our house; he's familiar with it and won't charge me an arm and a leg to come out." The man's voice replies. This must be the husband; even his voice sounds smaller than hers. Fuck, I just want to disappear, sneak out somewhere, my eyes searching frantically for a backdoor or some way out. They continue to talk as I hear them walking through the kitchen area, a wall separating us. They will be coming through this way and will surely see my dumb ass standing here.

"Yeah, I understand that, but it's the first I hear about it. It could have waited until the weekend, I'm sure." She says with an uncomfortable laugh, and I hear footsteps coming. Could I make it out the front door before they round the corner? The footsteps get louder, and I panic, opening the door at my back.

Swinging open the door, I see a flight of stairs leading down into a basement. Slowly, trying to make my footfalls as light as possible, I creep down the stairs, taking in the large open space of the basement. Reaching the bottom step, I see the clean and organized open area. Containers line the back wall, full of decorations for each season, I'm sure. I stop to listen for their footsteps above me when I hear the basement door open. What the fuck?

Seeing a row of locker-style cabinets, I frantically open them looking for a place to hide. I am destined to be caught tonight; I should have never come into this fucking house. Finding a closet on the far side of the basement that is empty enough to fit into, I shove my body in and listen to the conversation of the two people now in the basement with me. How the fuck did I manage to get myself stuck in this situation?

"Where is this crack in the foundation? I don't see anything. Are you sure you're not overreacting? You tend to do that from time to time." Shelli's voice bounces off the basement walls, condescending and annoyed. I can see them perfectly from the crack in the closet door. I watch her roll her eyes at this man as he gestures to the wall on the far side of the basement.

"Look right here; it trails all the way down. Look." He points to the containers I saw when I first came down. I realize that I will have to wait until they leave and go to bed before I can make my escape. Hopefully, this won't take too long. I should have taken the chance and made a run for it out the front door. Now, I'm going to be stuck in this cramped closet for god knows how long. I watch as she leans over a stack of containers, her ass looking just as good from the closet door as it does swaying down the street. I almost don't even realize the man is backing away, slowly picking up a baseball bat from the side of the wall. What is he doing? I ask myself the question, but I already know the answer. My mind just can comprehend fast enough as I watch her bending over, looking for this crack in the foundation he claims is there; she doesn't notice the man approaching with the bat. Covering my mouth, I want to yell out to warn her, but I can't give up my position.

Forcing my eyes shut and my hand over my mouth, I hear the crack as it no doubt hits Shelli. When I finally open my eyes, I see her body go limp and fall to the floor. Oh my god, did he just kill her? I thought my heart was racing before, but now it's about to beat out of my chest. I fear that he will be able to hear it from where I'm hiding in the closet. My stomach turns as I watch him drag her body across the floor to a beam where he chains her up. What the fuck am I witnessing here? How can this be happening? The man I once thought was some pussywhipped douchebag just assaulted his wife. I'm trapped in a fucking closet witnessing it; I can't do anything. My body wants to burst out of this closet and tackle him for what he's done to her. I may be a worthless piece of shit, but one thing I don't do and never have done is put my hands on a woman. I want to be the man I know I should be and do something to save her, but I hear my daddy's voice over the thrashing in my ears. I knew he was right; as I stand here frozen in this closet, I'm just a pussy.

Three loud knocks coming from above have my head looking up to the ceiling and out to see this man's reaction. Someone else is here; someone will see what he's done, the crime he's committed. I won't be stuck here for long because this piece of shit is going to jail. I watch as the man checks that Shelli is chained up nicely, then kicks her feet behind the pillar. Looking up to the ceiling, he smiles while opening a small black box on a shelf to the right. My eyes widen as I watch him pull out a gun and tuck it into his waistband. Any chance of me charging after him is gone now that I know he has a gun?

"Your little boyfriend is here. Now it's a party." He slaps duct tape across her mouth as he kicks her legs again, ensuring she is fully hidden behind this pillar. Should I yell? I could scream and alert whoever is at the front door that we are trapped down here. But he grabbed a gun for a reason; he wasn't going to let anyone interfere with what he had planned. Running my hands through my sweaty hair, I hear a moan from across the room; I watch as Shellli starts to stir but doesn't make another sound. At least she isn't dead yet. What started out as a fear of getting caught has now become a fear of being killed. Tears stream down my face as I wipe them furiously away. I should be helping her; I should be doing something. Instead, I'm crying and hiding like a little kid in a closet. Flashbacks to my childhood shake me to my core, and I try to push past the memory. The memory of me having to hide from the drunken ass-whoopings, hiding in the closet, praying I'm not found. The memory makes my body shake. I want desperately to get the fuck out of here.

But what the fuck am I supposed to do. I can't leave, not yet. This maniac will be back soon, and I can only hope whoever is at the door is someone that can help us. I slow my breathing, almost holding my breath as I hear the conversation from upstairs. Footsteps sound across the ceiling as it leads to the basement. I fight the urge to scream out when I hear the door open. Each step causes more panic as the man comes down the stairs, and I can hear him talking about the foundation.

"I'm glad you came over to check it out. I appreciate it. Shelli seems to think it's not important or that I'm overreacting, but in your experience, I'm sure you understand why I was so concerned when I saw it. I mean, a crack in the foundation of anything is detrimental. A house, a relationship, even a friendship. I mean, the foundation is everything." The man rambles on but doesn't sound nervous at all about another person possibly stumbling on the crime he committed. My eyes squint as I try to listen and understand why he sounds almost excited to have this man here.

The guy walks into my line of view, short and stocky, dressed casually. His body language looks apprehensive, but he follows along.

"Yeah, I mean, I don't mind at all. I have seen a crack in the foundation ruin a home. It's not something to ignore for sure." He replies as he and this monster stand in the middle of the basement. From where he stands, he can't see what horror awaits him behind that pillar. My eyes widen as I watch him point to where the body is lying. "It's over there," he gestures to a wall. I can't believe what I'm seeing. Does he want to get caught? Why are we still talking about this crack in the foundation bullshit? What is going on? He is leading this guy right to the body of Shelli, which is still lying motionless on the floor.

"How dangerous is a crack in the foundation," he asks as the man makes his way toward the wall about to discover the body. I can't take my eyes off the scene that is unfolding in front of me.

"Oh, very dangerous and costly, my friend." This guy says before his feet stop abruptly as he sees the body. Turning around, he is met by the man holding him at gunpoint. I wait to hear the shot's echo, but when it doesn't come, all I hear is his voice.

"How dangerous is it when you fuck your friend's wife. How expensive is that crack in the foundation?" he says, still pointing the gun at this man's head. Holy Shit, this just got interesting, and now I know I might never get out of here.

Chapter Five

The scene unfolds in front of me, and I can't help but feel like I'm being pranked. Did someone see me come into the house and decide to teach the thief a lesson? I pray for the moment they turn around and yell, "Come on out. We got you," but that moment doesn't come. Instead, I am watching as this man puts his hands up, pleading for his life while held at gunpoint. I'm sweating; my body feels like it's on fire as I wait for the gunshot to ring our ears.

The man with the gun doesn't look nervous at all holding the gun out with a stiff, confident arm like he's done this before. My hands would be trembling if I ever held someone else's life in them like he is now. One tiny squeeze of a finger and this man's life will end right before my eyes. My lip shakes as I try to suck in a quiet breath, keeping my location hidden from this madness.

"Please, Eric. Come on, man. Let's talk about this." The man pleads with a shaky voice. Now I know the psychopath's name is Eric. Eric still holds the gun steady while shaking his head at every word the man says. Where was this confidence before when I watched these people for over a week? This man seemed weak and mousey, submitting to his wife's every beck and call. What some people would have called a "yes man," but now that man is gone. I don't see that same submissive demeanor. Has he snapped?

Shelli starts to move slowly, finally coming back into consciousness. She resembles a child just waking up, forgetting they fell asleep on the sofa. She stares blankly for a moment before she realizes where she is and how she got there. I can feel the panic stemming from her from across the room as she pulls against the chains.

"What the fuck is going on. Eric?" she yells, then looks confused at the man being held at gunpoint. "Wait, Hanson? What is going on? Oh my god, Eric, put the gun down. What are you doing?" She starts to pull on her restraints again, her voice cracking with anxiety. The corner of Eric's mouth tilts up in a cynical smirk as he hears this anxiety in her voice. Knowing the tables have turned, I'm sure he is sick with power.

From what I have gathered from this terrifying episode I'm watching from the luxury of this cramped closet, is that Shelli has been fucking his friend, Hanson, behind his back. I'm sure that has to sting the ego a bit, but even I don't think it deserves this type of punishment. She's a beautiful woman, an unfaithful little vixen, as it turns out. You cut your losses and move on; you don't kill the fucking woman. There has to be more to this than what's going on. Now, I really do feel like I'm watching a movie play out before my eyes, one that I didn't buy tickets to see. I'm forced to watch this shit when all I wanted to do was be balls deep inside Mikki by now with these god-forsaken panties to my nose. Nothing ever goes the way I want it to; I'm always dealt the shit hand. That's why I never took up gambling, because I'm poor as shit and the most unlucky son of a bitch there is.

"Eric, calm down. We can explain; this isn't what you want to do." Shelli's voice sounds smaller than I have ever heard it sound. She knows she's truly fucked up, and it will be a miracle if any of us make it out of this basement tonight.

"Hanson, be a pal and go ahead and tie yourself up." Eric flicks the gun toward the other set of restraints, smiling the whole time. Hanson is frozen but no longer pleading; he looks like he might be sick.

"You planned this all out, didn't you? You're going to kill us?" Hanson asks, not moving at all. Now, I'm the one begging silently from across the room. Please just fucking listen to him; he's obviously not right in the head.

"Well, I'm going to have a little fun first. Why should only you two have all the fun, right? Now move." Eric shoves the gun in the direction again. I let out a silent gush of air as Hanson slowly moves toward the restraints. I can see from his body language that, just like me, he is judging if he can make it to the basement door without being caught, in his case, without catching a bullet in his ass. My legs are starting to cramp at the odd angle that I must stand to see what's happening. I wait till Hanson is jingling the chains, restraining himself, to risk adjusting my cramped position. I allow the scrapping of the chains against the concrete floor to mask any sound I might have made.

"Eric, please. You don't want to do this. This is crazy, right? You know this is insane. Please. I won't say anything about this. We can work this out. I can leave if you want me to. Just let's talk, ok?" Shelli begs on her knees now, pulling at the chains on her wrists. I can tell she is trying to sound as soft and convincing as possible to get out of this situation.

"You can't leave," Eric answers, looking shocked that she would even offer to do that. "You want me to let you leave and act like none of this happened? I gave up my entire life for you. I turned my back on my family; I moved across the fucking country for you. You think I'm just going to let you walk out that door?" He continues as his voice gets louder and louder. He wears a look of "how dare you" on his face like she must be the crazy one. This woman must have really done a number on him. I almost feel sorry for the poor bastard. He paces the floor like a lion as he continues yelling until he stops and points the gun right at her head.

"Or, I know; you think I'm going to let you keep fucking my friend behind my back? You have a way of manipulating every fucking person in your life. If I let you talk enough, I'm sure you could convince me I'm the crazy one. I'm the one overreacting when you've been letting this piece of shit fuck you!" He yells, and I cringe at his words. Finally, his confidence falters, and his voice shakes with emotion. He's angry and hurt beyond belief. She shakes her head, crying out, pleading for forgiveness. I don't think she deserves his forgiveness, but I still don't think she's earned a death sentence from it. I knew she was probably a real bitch, but she has mentally fucked this guy sideways. Love will make you do some crazy shit, and I'm seeing proof of that right now.

Women stay with men who treat them like dirt under their boots. I'm not sure whether that's from fear or love, but they stay. They stick around because they love the mean old bastards and hope he will change one day. Love is not always a good thing. It can feel really good when it's good, but when it's bad, well, it can kill you. I say a silent gratitude for my arrangement with Mikki, simple and to the point. We both stay around each other long enough for the parts that feel good, but she's out the door before it can go any further. I like that; I appreciate that kind of love because god help me if I ever had to feel what this man is going through right now. He's lost his fucking mind over this woman. I almost laugh to myself because I'm not so different, am I? Here I am, trapped in a fucking closet with a pair of panties and perfume in my pocket. I'll probably die with the shit still weighing down my jeans with a bullet in my ass. I'm in this predicament because I became obsessed with the scent of this woman; I can't imagine how I would act if I ever actually dipped my dick in her. This man is batshit crazy, but I understand him just a little more now.

Chapter Six

"Look, I'm sorry, man. Let her go; you and I can talk this out like men. This isn't you, Eric. You know that." Handson says as he adjusts himself against the restraints. He is probably the most guilty of all of these people, in my opinion. That's your friend's wife, man; you don't do that. Everyone knows that the wife is off-limits. What if she came onto him, though? I shake my head because why am I even trying to get myself sucked into this soap opera. This shit isn't any of my business, and me sticking my nose in it will only make it worse. I don't care who fucked who; I just need to get the fuck out of here. I'm feeling restless, and my chest gets tighter.

"No, this is the new me, the me that sets boundaries. The me that refuses to let everyone walk all over him. I'm done. The constant fucking gaslighting and making me seem like I'm overreacting when it's her, it's you, it's my boss, it's all of you. The minute someone finally stands up for themselves, oh no, he's crazy. No fuck that." Eric yells the confidence back in his voice.

"I've known about you two for weeks. Yeah, but I'm so conditioned to not causing a scene, trying to make up excuses for you both in my head until, finally, something clicked. I was going to kill myself; I still might. But all the puzzle pieces finally snapped into place, and I realized if I was going to die anyway, I might as well get my revenge, right? I'm going to have some fun." Eric finishes his rant and walks over to check the restraints. A sickening feeling starts to creep up into my chest; this is about to get really bad. I can sense it. If he was going to kill them, he would have just shot them already. What does he mean when he says he's about to have some fun? What does he have planned? That restless feeling starts to turn into panic as I watch him move around the basement.

"I understand you are upset. You have every right to be. But killing us won't help anything." Shelli begs between sobs; I can see the snot running down her face, glistening in the light. A woman I have seen walk with such confidence and power now looks pathetic.

"What don't you understand? I have nothing to lose. You took me from my family, and then you took the only friend I had out here. You took him, and you fucked him, in our car, in our fucking house." I flinch as he kicks her, as if his foot hit me instead.

"Fuck, man, stop. Please just let her go. I came on to her. I made the first move. It's my fault." Hanson pleads with tears falling from his eyes. His chest rises and falls quickly as if holding in giant sobs.

"Look at you; another man is begging to save your life. He is willing to throw everything away for you too. What is it? Magic? What about you makes us want to throw our lives away for you? The pussy isn't that good, so it must be magic." Eric laughs, looking at her in disgust. "No, I'm done; I'm not under your spell anymore." He sounds like a man, so sure of what he will do; it is terrifying. Suddenly, he looks around the room, and my heart sinks. I back up in a rush, trying not to fall over in the small space, scared he might see me. The only sound I hear is the pathetic whimpers coming from Shelli. What if my body cast a shadow, or what if he saw me in the small crack in the door? I wait, holding my breath, hoping the doors don't swing open, revealing my hiding spot this whole time.

"Damn, I had this all planned out in my head, and now that I got you here, I'm too excited. I don't know what to start with first." Hearing his voice has me clutching my chest. Fuck he could have seen me. I need to be careful. I stay back a little further and look out, watching as he has his hands on his head and is looking around the basement for something.

"There are so many options, right?" he sounds so excited and happy, as if he isn't about to commit murder. "I have to be honest; I did my research. Did you know, long ago, they would torture a person by what they called a Judas cradle? Yeah, it was a pillar with a pyramid on top. They would strip the person naked and sit them on the pyramid. They would then use a rope to pull down the person's limbs daily. The idea was to stretch them until they split open or died from infection. But that was so long ago. If I had the time, I would have loved to fix something up like that for you, honey. I know how much you hated the idea of ass-play. So being able to stretch you out before you die had me rock solid. But that's ok. I have other ideas." He laughs, opening a box with his back turned. I surprise myself when I shrug my shoulders; I do like some ass-play. I am grateful he didn't have the time to create whatever contraption he was talking about. I don't think I could watch someone be split apart through their asshole. This guy is into some fucked up shit. Which has my mind reeling, thinking of what exactly he has planned for these two. What will I have to watch happen? I could close my eyes, cover my ears, but it's hard to look away when the devil is right in front of you.

"You need help, man. Let us go, and we can get you help." Hanson begs.

"Help? I don't need help. I needed my friend not to fuck my wife behind my back." He says matter of factly. Turning around, he holds a nail gun, admiring it like a new toy. My stomach sinks again, and they both start to scream. He's fucking with them; he's just trying to scare them. There is no way he will use that on them. Shelli and Hanson are screaming for help, and I want to join them; I don't want to see whatever this sick fuck has planned. The urge to scream, "Let me out of here," is on the tip of my tongue.

"Hey, hey, now you don't even know what I'm going to do yet. Now who is overreacting?" He smiles at them; he really is enjoying this. I watch as he adjusts the dials and checks to ensure it's loaded with nails. My brain is flipping through all the ways he could use this damn thing on these people. I know the pain of getting a nail through the foot; I stepped on one when I was younger. I remember running barefoot in the yard when a sharp, searing pain stopped me in my tracks. I fell down and got to wailing so loud; Daddy came out of the house yelling. Instead of coming to check on me, he made me get up and limp to the back porch where he was waiting, annoyed with my existence. I could see the rusty nail sticking through the bottom of my foot, blood pooling around the edges; it hurt so damn bad.

Daddy just rolled his eyes and yanked that fucker out so hard I threw up right then and there. I got in trouble for that too. I can remember that pain like it was yesterday; it's not pleasant at all.

"You're fucking crazy! Let us go!" Shelli yells, anger dripping from each word. I shake my head because I know you never tell a crazy person they are crazy. They don't like that; it upsets them.

"You have no idea just how crazy things are going to get, my love" Eric's words strike fear in us all as he steps closer to Shelli. Nail gun through the head? No, that would be too quick; he would have just shot her if he wanted that. Maybe he will just shoot her in the hand or something. Fuck, my stomach turns at each scenario that plays out in my mind. No matter what, this shit is about to hurt. I'm not sure I can watch it.

"Oh, I almost forgot." Eric holds up a finger and goes to a container he has open. Pulling out a set of small tongs, he waves them at her.

"Can't forget these." He walks back over to Shelli with the nail gun in one hand and these tongs in the other. What the fuck does he need that for?

"Get on your knees, Shelli. Come on, babe, one last time for me." He laughs and pokes out his bottom lip.

"No, what are you going to do? Please, please stop." Her voice is rough from screaming as she tries to move, and the chains rattle. Hanson goes to move closer to protect her, but his hands are bound. I can't do anything from where I stand. All I can do is hope and pray to a god I don't believe in that someone, anyone, heard their screams.

"You have gotten on your knees for him several times. Come on, just like before." He points the nail gun at her head.

"NOW!' He yells as she scrambles to move to her knees.

"Ok, ok fuck!" she cries. I shut my eyes, but they open again almost instantly. Why can't I stop watching this? Does watching this all happen make me guilty also? I'm standing here doing nothing, but what am I supposed to do? He would shoot me dead the minute I opened this closet door. I watch as Shelli gets on her knees, hands restrained behind her back in front of Eric. My mind is still searching for some idea of what he is about to do to this woman.

"Now I sharpened the tips for these nails, so it should be quick and almost painless, for you at least. Stick out your tongue." Eric says, and I feel the room start to get smaller. Please, god, no.

Chapter Seven

She cries, snot dripping, and I realize I'm crying with her. I wipe away the tears of frustration pooling in my eyes. He won't go through with it, right?

"Open wide, baby; you can do it. I've seen it. Stick out your tongue." She slowly sticks out her tongue, her body shaking in fear. Clamping the end of her tongue with the small tongs, he pulls, stretching her soft pink tongue out of her mouth. I can hear her gagging and crying over Hanson's pleas. Eric places the small nail gun under her tongue with one hand while pulling the tongs with the other. A brief moment of silence fills the basement as if we all were holding our breaths in the hopes that he wouldn't do it. Then, he sends the first nail up through the bottom of her tongue, and the room erupts in screams. I cover my ears, but my eyes are glued to the scene. I can see the sharp tip of the nail shining in the fluorescent light above her head. She screams the most gut-wrenching scream, and he holds on tight to the clamp.

"Don't move, honey. I wouldn't want to miss." He sends another through the bottom of her tongue. Blood mixed with saliva falls from her mouth as he continues his assault. I lost count of the number of times he sent the small nails through the bottom of her swollen tongue. Finally, he lets her go once her tongue is full of sharp tips. Her tongue hangs heavy out of her mouth. "See, it wasn't that bad. Right?" He pets her head. Her tongue looks like one of those wooden bats with all the spikes you see in movies. The top of her tongue is full of small, shiny, sharp tips as it hangs out of her mouth, dripping more blood and saliva down her chin.

"Now, Hanson, I know your hands are tied, so I'll help a friend out. Stand up." He says. I feel like I'm going to be sick as I swallow to make sure I don't vomit in this closet.

"Fuck man, come on." Hanson is crying harder now, and I don't blame him. Eric doesn't waste time putting the nail gun to his head.

"Come on, don't ruin the fun. You're going to love this part." Eric says with that sadistic smile. Hanson pulls on his chains, one last attempt to escape the chains holding him hostage before he stands up. Is he going to nail-gun his tongue too?

I cover my mouth and swallow the rising bile when Eric bends down and unbuckles Hanson's pants. I know where this is going, and the vomit rises again as I force it down. God, please, don't let this happen. Let me out of here! Eric pulls down Hanson's pants with his boxers, exposing his dick.

"Wow, really? You chose this over me? Maybe he's a grower and not a shower, but I think I at least got him beat on girth." He laughs out loud while Shelli continues to cry.

"Fuck you," Hanson barks out in anger, and I wish he could break out of those chains. I wish he could break out and turn the gun on this sick fuck. I don't want to see what comes next.

"Ok, I don't think I have to explain this too much. Shelli, do what you do best and suck his dick." Eric explains, and Shelli begins shaking her head, pleading under her breath.

"Show me what I couldn't see when you both were in the car that one time. Remember, not too long ago, you went to grab something from the office, and instead, you went to the park. I'm pretty sure what happened when you jumped in his parked car, right? Show me." Eric insists as he holds up the nail gun again. He planned this all out so perfectly. This man knew the length of nails to use so that the sharp tips would stick out of her tongue just enough to shred his dick. He knew the velocity to set the nail gun to so that it pierced the tongue without going all the way through. This was not some man who just snapped; no, this was premeditated. For weeks, he has been planning his revenge on these people, and now my stupid ass gets to witness this brutal torture.

" I can't," Shelli gags, tongue still hanging and out, slurring her words.

" I can't understand a word you are saying. You really should do what I ask. I would hate to cut our time together short." Eric steps closer, putting the nail gun against her head as she panics.

" Ok, ok, please don't." She cries as she pulls against the chains coming closer to Hanson. How did he know how long to make the chains? How did he know how to set this up so they could reach each other? Every single detail was thoughtfully planned out.

"No, no, no, please. Fuck, I'm sorry! No, don't do this."Hanson starts to panic, seeing the jagged pieces of nails sticking out through her tongue. Shelli whispers her apologies before she moves her head side to side, trying to get his limp dick into her mouth without using her hands. Hanson hisses in pain as she fumbles but finally gets his cock in her mouth.

"Faster, really get into it. I know you can do better than that." Eric instructs her as she struggles to do what he's demanding. She shakes her head, letting go as Hanson's body shakes.

"Eric, please," Shelli slurs with a swollen tongue, trying to plead again. Please, man, end this. At this point, I wish he would just shoot them both and be done with this. My prayers go unanswered when he takes the nail gun and shoots her in the thigh. She screams so loud my ears ring from across the room.

" I said now, or the next one is through your fucking skull. You didn't mind shoving his dick down your throat a week ago. You didn't mind at all, so fucking do it now." Eric roars, his patience wearing thin.

She shakes her head, trying to apologize, but it comes out gargled. She moves her head around, bending and flinching with the nail now in her thigh as she attempts to get his cock back into her mouth. I can tell once she has the limp meat in her mouth because Hanson's eyes widen, and he begins to scream. I don't even realize I am holding my own dick in my hand, wincing in pain. I can almost feel his pain in my dick as I try to hold down the vomit that has been threatening to come up. Shelli's cheeks suck in as she tightens her lips to keep his dick from spilling out, shoving the nails deeper into his flesh. Screams fill the basement with each jerking move of her head. I gag, but no one can hear me as I try to keep myself from hurling. Blood pours from the sides of her mouth as she moves faster, gagging and crying. Hanson stomps his feet in pain, his knees bending, almost giving out. Eric watches with a zoned-out smile on his face. I can't tell if he's angry or amused. Suddenly he snaps out of it and shakes his head.

"Ok, ok, enough." He kicks her off of him, as she falls backward. I'm sick and sweating while looking at her bloody mouth. Chunks of meat hang on the tips of the sharp edges sticking out of her tongue. Hanson's cries have into silent gasps of air. I'm surprised he hasn't passed out yet.

"Man, you should see your dick right now. Were you not circumcised?" Eric asks while Hanson shakes and cries.

"Yes? No? Well, if not, you are now." He laughs, clapping his hands and slapping him on the shoulder.

" That was intense. Man, I think I even got a semi here." Eric rubs the front of his pants like this shit may really arouse him. He turns back to the box of goodies pulling out a thin metal rod. What can he possibly do now? Just put these people out of their misery so that I can get the fuck out of here! I fight the urge to put my fist through the closet wall. The frustration of being trapped and forced to be a witness to his morbid crimes is boiling over, and I'm not sure how much more I can take.

Shelli gets back onto her knees as she lean over, and the sounds of her vomit hits the cement floor. The chunky liquid falls from her mouth, dripping off the ends of her mangled tongue.

"Damn it, Shelli; you always have to be so fucking dramatic, don't you." Eric shakes his head at her, clearly annoyed by her sickness, before turning back to Hanson.

" I have to say I didn't think she would do such a number on your dick, but I think you have some good tissue left over. Look, I know there is a lot of pressure on you right now, man, but I need you to get hard for me." He says, and Hanson's eyes turn up to the ceiling, defeated in his pain, he starts to pray. Eric ignores his prayers and continues.

"Her skills are subpar; trust me, I understand, but this next part really needs a stiff one." He says, patting Hanson on the back as Hanson's eyes widen and his face squints in anger and pain.

"Come on, she wasn't that bad, right? Think of all the times you had her in the car or that time in her office. Surly that could get you hard right." Eric lifts Hanson's shirt, and I get dizzy as I finally see the result of Shelli's suck job. The closet gets even smaller as I see the hanging strips of raw, red meat that used to be this man's dick. Blood drips from each piece of hanging flesh, and I swallow my vomit for the third time. Eric makes a show of flapping Hanson's mangled dick.

"NO? That's alright. I'll help you out. What are friends for, right?" Eric grabs his dick with one hand, placing the metal rod at the tip of the head. "Deep breath, buddy," Eric warns before he pushes the metal rod into the tiny hole of his dick. The room spins, and the screams sound muffled as I fight not to lose consciousness. Someone help me.

Chapter Eight

Eric forces the rod through his dick right before Hanson falls to his knees. Shaking my head, I fight to pull the air into my lungs. I want to cry and sit down, but I can't. My legs hurt, my chest is tight, and I need to look away. But looking at the blank walls has my claustrophobia peaking, and this crack in the door is the only thing keeping the walls from closing in completely. After taking a step back, Eric looks at his handwork.

"Well, that will work. Look at that." Eric sounds pleased as he admires the mangled meat surrounding the metal rod he forced into Hanson's dick.

"Now, this next part is a little rough," he says, wasting no time grabbing the nail gun; he goes to work on impaling the flesh with nails. A short clicking sound can be heard when each nail hits the metal rod.

Hanson's screams sound raw and hoarse as he looks like he may pass out. I force myself to look away. I can't watch this shit; I need a break. Sobs follow each soft air sound of the nail gun and that soft clinking sound. When the nail gun stops, I look up through eyes blurred with tears. Like Shelli's tongue, Hanson's dick looks like some medieval spiked weapon.

"Ribbed for her pleasure, right?" He snickers and then turns, pointing his finger at Shelli. She shakes her head and tries backing away as Eric moves forward, nodding his head.

" No, no, please, help," her mutilated tongue, slurring her words. She screams and starts coughing, chunks of vomit and blood spewing from her panicked mouth. My knees give out when I realize what he has planned. I'm able to right myself back up quickly, but not before my knees hit the closet door slightly. I might pass out, but now I am fully on alert because the sound causes Eric's back to stiffen. He looks around the basement as I hold my breath. That is it; I fucked up, and I'm caught. He looks over at Hanson and decides it must have been him who made the noise as he turns back to Shelli. I hate to say I am grateful he has his attention back on them, but I am. I don't want to be tortured like this. My adrenaline flows like electricity through my veins at how close I was to being caught.

"What am I doing? This is sick." Eric's voice sounds shaky as he seems to zone out, dropping the nail gun and moving his hands on his head. Everyone is stunned and silent for a moment. What is happening? God, do you really exist? Have you finally heard my prayers, you lazy fuck! I watch in stunned silence as he paces back and forth.

"I'm crazy; I've fucking lost it." He lets out a shaky breath, and both Hanson and Shelli are stunned for a moment, probably shock finally setting in. Between shaky breaths and cries, they look at each other and back to Eric. He rushes toward Shelli, getting on his knees, and she flinches.

"Honey, I'm so sorry. Fuck look at you. What have I done?" Eric's voice sounds so sincere, as if he is waking up from a bad dream. Eyes wide, Eric panics and starts to unchain Shelli's hands, freeing her.

Hanson's body falls in what might be relief or loss of blood. Eric cries as he hugs her, and Shelli's body relaxes into his embrace. I still can't come out of this closet; it might throw him back into whatever psychosis he was in. My face is wet with tears and sweat as relief floods my body. I know they won't forgive him or let him get away with this, but maybe, just maybe, they will leave this basement and give me a chance to get the fuck out of here. God, I will never lie or steal ever again. Fuck, I may even start going to church, and this time, I won't steal out of the charity basket.

All I have to do is wait until they get out of here, and I'll be free to go. I watch as Eric lets go of Shelli, then places both hands on the side of her face, looking deep into her eyes.

"I can't believe you are that fucking stupid." His words make my heart feels like it has a studder. What the fuck did he just say? Shaking my head in disbelief, I watch as he puts the gun under her chin and forces her back towards Hanson. No way, you fucking asshole. Don't do this. Please, no. This is supposed to be over. Looking up, I curse god for the sick joke he played.

How could I ever believe he would come through for me?

" Lay down and spread them, honey." He smiles, and all hope is gone. I don't wipe away the tears as they pour down my cheeks. I can't do this anymore. Eric pulls Hanson up onto his knees.

" I can't; please make it stop." Hanson cries as he is pushed to kneel between Shelli's trembling legs.

"Oh, you can; I've seen you do it a few times. I mean, I even put the rod there to help you. Now fuck my wife, Hanson. You have no problem fucking her behind my back, fuck her now." He stands behind Hanson undoing his chains, quickly putting the gun back to his head, and stepping back.

"Times ticking, Hanson." Eric steps forward, nudging Hanson's head with the gun barrel. Shelli nods to Hanson, and they share apologies again before he thrusts his mangled spiked dick into her as she screams. Still standing behind Hanson with the gun to the back of his head, Eric moves closer to watch.

"Look at me, Shelli, look me in the eyes while he fucks you. Look at me!" he yells as she screams and tries her best to stare at him. Blood pools around her as Hanson thrusts, both screaming in pain.

"Yeah, you like that? That pain you feel, that's how I felt watching you fucking betray me." He yells over her screams of agony. Looking down, I cover my ears, and the realization that I will never make it out of here sets in deep. Then the loud bang comes and forces me to look again. Hanson's head is splattered across Shelli and the wall behind her. Eric stands behind what's left of Hanson before the body slumps forward onto Shelli. She frantically pulls herself out from Hanson, screaming, and she pulls him out of her mangled pussy. Grabbing her stomach in pain, she crawls to the wall, glancing back at the blood and brain fragments as they slide down to the floor.

"How's that for a climax? Right?" Eric laughs. Her cries have turned into howls as she looks at herself and Hanson. Frantically wiping her arms and body, she looks insane from where I stand. There is no coming back from any of this. Anyone who is lucky enough to leave this room will never be the same. Eric stares at her, squinting his eyes in disgust as she howls Hanson's name.

"I wonder if you would have cried for me like this. If instead of doing all this, I just swallowed that gun. Would you have mourned for me, Shelli? Would you? Or would you both have been happy to finally be able to move on with each other now that I was out of the way." He starts to sound sad, almost childlike. Shelli looks up with eyes of pure rage.

"I could never fucking mourn for you because I quit loving you a long time ago, you fucking psycho." She yells at him, still slurring. I stand defeated, watching all this unfold. He squats down, and she curls into a ball, holding her stomach, no doubt feeling the pain from her insides being torn apart.

"Let's talk," Eric says before throwing his body toward her and bracing her head in his arms. She fights a little, but he holds her head, mouth open like he's fighting a dog that has something in its mouth. She pushes against his arms as he starts pulling the nails out of her tongue one by one. Finally, he lets her go, and she falls back against the wall, exhausted in pain. Standing up, he wipes his hands on his pants and looks down at her.

"When did you quit loving me, Shelli? Was it the day I disowned my mother because you claimed she never really liked you and she was going to tear us apart? No, that can't be it. Was it the day I moved thousands of miles away from my family and friends and bought you this house? No, that can't be it, either. Oh, I know, it must have been the day I found all those text messages in your phone from my brother-in-law. When I confronted you, and you convinced me it was all my fault. I was working too much, and he came on to you. I should have killed you that day. I should have cut the fucking cancer you are out of my life that day. But no, instead, we moved here and agreed on a fresh start. How is it, honey? Is this the fresh start you wanted?" He asks, leaning down to get back into her face.

This isn't the first time she's been unfaithful; this has been going on for a long time. I make no excuses for the monster that moves outside these closet doors, but I almost understand him. I heard once that there aren't bad people, but bad things that happen to people that make them bad. We all start off clean then life dirties us up. Every relationship shapes us into the person we are; in my case, it started with my parents. This woman emotionally tortured this man, some people can't handle it, and they snap. As I said, it's no excuse for the amount of sick torture that went on in this fucking basement. No one deserves these deranged forms of revenge. Hell, I could have snapped plenty of times and gotten my revenge on all the people that hurt me, but you just don't do that. I honestly don't have the stomach for it. People don't just snap for no reason, though; this woman must have fucked with this man's head. Still, she can't be all that bad to deserve this.

"Fuck you. You were a spineless mommy boy; you would have had me stuck in that town, being a part of the family. All of you are so pathetic. If I had to sit through another Sunday dinner, I was going to fucking off myself." She grits her teeth and spits each word out with venom.

"There we go; now we are getting some honesty, finally. Keep it coming." He urges her on, and I brace myself because she looks like she is really about to give it to him. The look on her face is pure evil.

"You want honesty? I fucked Will, oh yeah, your precious brother-in-law. I let him finger fuck me in your mother's house, too, while you all sat around the table, cackling and praising each other. The fakest fucking displays of affection. All of you were blind to what was really going on. No one is perfect, but you all pretended to be so goddamn hard. I made it a point to show all of you that none of you are better than me." She howls in pain as she sits up, and suddenly, I stand corrected.

This is an evil bitch.

Chapter Nine

"I knew I could find a crack in your perfect little family picture, so I fucked Will. Your sister with her perfect marriage, vacations, and the perfect little baby that everyone couldn't stop cooing at. Yeah, no one is perfect. I'm sure if I dug deep enough, I could have probably fucked your dad too." She starts laughing and hisses in pain. I stare out, waiting for him to kill her. I know it's coming. At this point, I want them to get this over with so I can leave; she can keep her panties and her perfume. I'll never be able to get the image of her choking on shredded cock out of my brain anyway. I feel stupid for getting myself into this situation over an evil bitch like this. Sure, I still feel sorry for her mangled snatch; maybe I'm just in shock, but I don't care anymore.

" Why? Why did you want to destroy my family? Destroy me? Why?" Eric shakes his head and sounds like he truly wants to know. I'm sure a good session with a marriage counselor could have fixed all this. Isn't that what rich folks do? They fuck around, then cry to some doctor about it.

"Because I know how it is to pose nicely for the family photo, then cry myself to sleep trying to block out the sounds of my dad beating the shit out of my mom. I know how it feels to smile in everyone's faces, then pray to a god that never listens when daddy is done with mommy and wants to visit his little girl in her bed. No one is perfect; no family is perfect. I wanted to be a part of your family, but they all looked at me like I was an outsider. They knew I would never fit into their perfect picture." She coughs and cries at the pain. As I said, bad things happen to people; then they turn into bad people. A fucked up childhood will really do a number on you. She continues as he stares at her with zero expressions. I'm sure he will kill her; it's just a matter of time before she dies anyway.

"I did love you once, but then I realized I loved the thought of you more. I was still chasing that perfect family picture. That's not the life I wanted, but you were so in love with me. You followed me around like a fucking puppy. You were there on the days I felt like chasing that dream, and Hanson and the others were the ones who were there when I knew it was all fake." She sits up with a shaky breath, blood and tissue pooling between her legs. I start to reflect on how I viewed this woman as a fancy painting in one of those museums. I always thought I would dirty her up if I touched her. Now, it sounds like she was always dirty. I may have even had a chance with her, but probably not. Glad I didn't, seeing as how this crazy motherfucker would have been on my tail. My stomach turns as I see the sticky blood pooling between her legs. I feel weak, dizzy, and defeated.

" If you're going to kill me, just fucking do it. In the end, I still win." She starts laughing again, and I'm surprised she is still breathing. She has lost so much blood.

"Look at what I've turned you into." Laughing and crying, she spits out more blood. He smiles at her like he has a secret to tell. He stands up, clapping his hands together.

"Yeah, well, I guess you're right. There is only one thing wrong with that. See, I still don't think you are a bad person. I think deep down inside; you have a heart. It's just that thing between your legs that's the problem. I have one more thing planned for you, my love. A sort of cleansing before you go." He goes back to the box and pulls out what looks like string and a bottle. My heart starts to pound in my ears again because I know this is it. She can't handle much more; there is no way she will survive any more of his torture. I know for a fact my stomach can't take much more. I squint to make out the label on the bottle. I recognize that bottle, red label with the tiny green cap, that's hot sauce. He stands in front of her shaking the bottle.

"Good old Louisiana hot sauce. It always feels like home. You know I put this shit on everything." He smiles and starts toward her. So he's a good old boy from Louisiana. I met a man on the street from there, and he was batshit crazy too.

"What the fuck are you doing" She starts to breathe faster as he approaches her. Grabbing her hair, he pulls her back toward the chains, and even with her putting up a fight, he manages to secure her wrists. Pulling the chains tighter, he has her hands over her head as he pulls her kicking legs to the chains he used on Hanson. Each leg restrained, he has her spread eagle, and I get a glimpse at the massacre between her legs. The contents of my stomach churn violently.

" I can't have you moving. This is a very careful procedure." Uncapping the bottle, he covers his hand in the red Tabasco sauce from his hometown. I stare in shock as he looks like he is using it to lather up his hands like soap, the red sauce dripping from his wrists. Bending down, he places one hand on her stomach, and the other dives into her mutilated pussy. Pumping fingers in and out of her pussy I can't tell what is blood and what is hot sauce. I can just smell the spicy scent in the air and hear the blood-curdling screams.

"Is this what turned you into the rotten bitch you are?" The sounds of blood squishing and her screams mix as he continues to finger fuck her, her legs shaking from the burning sensation. I can't handle this. For fucks sake, enough is enough.

" Now that we cleansed you let's sew this up," Holding a curved needle with dangling black string, he dives down and begins to sew with the needle and thread the lips of her pussy. I look away from him as his arms move and pull the thread tight before diving back in. You would swear this man was a fucking doctor sewing up the lips of her pussy with unshakable focus. A popping sound followed by a wet splatter interrupts her screams.

"You nasty fucking bitch" Eric stands up, backing away from her twitching body. She whimpers, but her screams are gone; she is dying. I look down to see what made him stop his torture, then the smell hits. A spicy mix of hot sauce and shit mingle with the metallic scent of blood in the air, and I can't hold it in anymore. She must have released her bowels in shock as the brown lumpy fluid mixes with the blood pooled between her legs. The most guttural retching sound leaves my body as I fold over, vomit pouring from my mouth. My eyes widen in fear because I know he hears me, but I can't stop the contents of my stomach from coming up.

Chapter Ten

Light pours into the once-dark space as the closet doors swing open. I'm still blowing chunks when my eyes look up to see Eric standing back with a look of shock and disgust.

"Who the fuck are you?" He asks, but the room is spinning from finally releasing the vomit that has been in my throat since this all started. Wiping my mouth on my sleeve, I step out of the closet; so many smells attack my nose, and I dry heave again, gripping my stomach. The room tilts and everything comes to a halt when I feel the gun press against my skull.

"I asked you a question, who the fuck are you?" Eric demands an answer, but I don't know what the fuck to say. I'm scared shitless, and I know he won't let me go. I have seen this man do the most vicious shit tonight to the people he once cared about. Can you imagine what he's about to do to me? A stranger caught in his house. Fuck it; I guess it's time to come clean.

"I'm sorry, man, I broke into the house. I was stupid. It was all a huge mistake. I won't say anything about what happened here. I'm just some bum; no one would believe me anyway. I'm a nobody." I plead with my hands up, hoping he doesn't pull the trigger. One squeeze of his finger, and I'm done. My heart is racing, waiting for the impact of the bullet. My life isn't flashing before my eyes like they say it does, and for that, I'm grateful.

"Wait, you broke into my house? Why are you in my fucking basement then?" He asks, confused and still pressing the gun to my head.

"I broke in to steal a few things. Then I was going to leave. But you guys came back, and I ran down here; I was going to leave once you all went to sleep or something." I try not to stutter my words.

"You have got to be kidding me. Talk about wrong place, wrong time." Eric drops the gun and starts laughing hysterically. I still hold my hands up for fear of putting them down. I watch as he wipes his tearful eyes from the belly laughs he gets from my fucked up situation.

"So, what exactly did you take? Did you even get anything? I mean, what kind of shitty luck do you have? You pick this house out of all the houses on the block? You've been in that closet the whole time?" he laughs again.

"Yeah, I know. Shitty luck, huh?" I offer an apprehensive laugh, but I'm about to piss myself.

"So, what did you take? Is my tv in that closet too? He smiles and crosses his arms.

"I ended up not taking anything. I don't want anything, man; I just want to leave." I say, hoping he is so fucked in the head he just lets me run out of here.

"Yeah, right, you must have taken something. Empty your pockets." He isn't smiling anymore. Fuck, I don't want to empty what's in my pockets. The panties and perfume feel like bricks weighing me down to where I stand.

"I just want to get out of here. I don't care about any of this. The unfaithful bitch had it coming, from what I understand. Ok? I just want to go." I'm trying to reason with a psychopath, and I can tell from the look on his face that it isn't working.

"I said, empty your pockets. Now." Eric yells, and I'm forced to reach into my pockets and pull out his wife's panties and a small perfume bottle. The shame I feel right now courses through me like a heat I've never felt before. This is where I meet my end. He yanks the panties out of my hands, then looks up at me, and I swear I'm looking the devil right in the eyes.

"This wasn't some random break-in. Was it? She's fucking you too?" Eric's lip curls up as if her fucking someone like me is the most disgusting thing he's ever heard. I can't say I disagree with him.

"No, No, No, I just saw her on the street. I told you I'm a fucking bum man; I beg people for money on the street. She passed me a few times, and I was fucking stupid. I got obsessed with the way she smelled. I know that sounds ridiculous. It is unbelievable, but I swear I never touched her. Fuck, I never even spoke to the bitch. I just wanted to get something that smelled like her. I'm sorry, I'm fucked up, ok?" I hear myself rambling, but I can't stop; my words, like vomit, pour out of me, hoping he understands. He stares at me like the pathetic piece of shit I am for a moment, letting me ramble and beg.

"I never touched her. I never touched her. " I repeat my words, hoping they stick somewhere in his fucked up brain. He looks down at his feet, almost like he is thinking about what to do next. I hope this means he is thinking of letting me run out of here. But when those evil eyes look up at me, I know it's just a matter of time before I join the carnage on the basement floor. Tears start to run down my face; I'm a blubbering mess because he starts to smile that smile I've seen several times tonight. I'm not leaving this basement. God, the least you can do is have him make it quick. You have been a real dickhead to me my whole life. Can you at least make my death quick? I don't want to be tortured like these people were tonight.

"You want to fuck my wife? " Eric's words stop my crying for a moment. I stare at him, wondering if I heard him correctly.

"No, no. I don't. I never did. That was never my intention." I explain as he starts to walk over to me. My asshole clenches up with each step he takes. My daddy would get a real kick out of how much of a pussy I am. I can just see him now.

"Sure you do. That's what led you here. Right? You said it was her what? Her smell?" He stops in front of me as I put my hands up.

"I never wanted to fuck her, never. I just want to leave. Please." I beg, shaking my head and crying like the pathetic idiot I am. I never should have been in this fucking house. I should have known better than to do what I did. I was a fool to believe for one second that I would make it out of this basement. I'll never drink another drink, feel the tension release with each bottle I empty. I'll never sink my dick into Mikki's crusty snatch or her tight little ass again. My pathetic life ends tonight.

"Well, I would hate for you to leave empty-handed or unfulfilled. It turns out me and the wife didn't quite work out. So, how about you go ahead and get what you really came for." He says, gripping the back of my neck and pushing me towards Shelli's body.

"No, please. I want to leave." I yell as he pushes me down to my knees in front of her mangled body. My pants sink into the warmth of blood and shit as I kneel between Shelli's wide-open legs. I try not to breathe in the mingling smells assaulting my nose. Shelli's weak moan surprises me; how is she still alive?

"That's what you came for, right there. That's what you really wanted. I made it extra tight for you." Eric grips the back of my neck again, forcing me to look at his handiwork. The black thread stands out against the swollen, bloody lips of her pussy.

"I can't. Please." I close my eyes, not wanting to look at her. The most beautiful woman I had ever seen now lies brutally beaten and tortured in front of me. The work of art I pictured her to be now torn to pieces. Holding the gun to my head, he bends down to my ear.

"Fuck her now, or I'll blow your worthless fucking brains out!" He yells in my ear, and the ringing follows. I unbuckle my pants, and they fall to the floor, now covered in shit and blood. I try to hide my flaccid dick, not wanting the same metal rod shoved down my piss hole. My body shakes as I close my eyes and tug on my dick, trying desperately to make it somewhat hard enough to do what this motherfucker wants. To my utter disgust and shock, my dick actually does get hard enough, and I'm not sure what that says about me. I know I deserve to die; I've done some fucked up shit. Nothing as bad as this guy, but I'm sure, to most standards, I've fallen short. Leaning forward, the head of my dick presses into the swollen flesh of Shelli's mutilated cunt. Her body jerks, and her eyes open, locking at mine, and I want to die right now. I'm ready to end this; I hate that she has to see me doing this to her. A popping sound follows as I finally get my dick past her sewn-up pussy lips. She starts to jerk and twitch violently as I sink my dick inside her.

"There you go. Is that what you came for?" Eric's voice is muffled in my mind due to my heartbeat thrumming in my ears. I thrust deeper, and my balls twitch; I hate that this feels so good. I am a fucking monster, a pathetic piece of shit. Shelli's screams mix with Eric's, but I hear nothing. I'm lost, zoned out in my mission to do what he says. It isn't until the metallic smell of blood and the rancid smell of shit wafts up with each thrust that I am pulled back into the present reality. My stomach tightens, forcing me to lean over in pain as the bile burns my throat. The yellow acidic fluid dribbles from my lips onto Shell'is stomach. The blood and bile mix onto her pale skin, the colors resembling an infected sore.

Sitting back up onto my ankles, I feel the gun press into the back of my head. I close my eyes as my heart races, dick still hard and dripping with enough bodily fluids to make me want to puke again. A sense of calm suddenly washes over me, knowing that is it.

"See you in hell, my love," Eric's voice is all I hear before the loud sound of the gun goes off. I feel the wet blood splatter hit my face, and I open my eyes to see he shot Shelli, a bullseye, right in her forehead. He didn't kill me. I look wide-eyed as he steps around, looking down at her body. I'm in shock; I know it. He doesn't look at me, and I can't move. He didn't kill me, the gun still in his hand at his side. I'm still frozen when he finally looks at me; I don't want to move.

"You got some blood on you. Right there." He says, pointing to my face where his wife's brain matter is surely spattered across it. I'm confused, but not for long, as he raises the gun to my face. A blinding light explodes in my vision before it all fades to black.

Epilogue

Standing in the basement, he looks over what he has done. Was it all worth it? He knows he will be caught, but he makes no attempts to cover his hellish actions as he makes his way up the basement steps. Closing the door behind him, he feels the clock ticking in his bones. He doesn't have much time to get out of here, and the drive back to Louisiana is a long one.

Walking upstairs, he enters the bedroom he once shared with the woman he thought was the love of his life. Instead, he realizes she was sent here by the devil himself to end his life. The mirror in the bathroom shows the bloody reflection of a man pushed to his limits for years until finally, tonight, he broke. He washes his hands and face; the blood of three different people turns the sink pink as he washes them off. He looks up at himself in the mirror, and a sense of peace washes over his expression. He has no remorse or regrets for what he's done tonight. She will never ruin another man's life like she did his. He changes his clothes and combs his hair.

Grabbing a duffle bag, he packs a few pairs of clothes, his toothbrush, and his mouthwash. The bag is light with the last few things he will need until the police catch up with him. It won't take them long to find the massacre downstairs and to know it was all his doing. He planned on ending his life with all of them in that basement, but he realized what he needed to do after hearing Shelli's rants.

Closing the door to the house, he throws the duffle bag over his shoulder as he walks to the SUV. The street is quiet, no one knowing what lies in the basement of his house. Everyone is living their lives oblivious to the bloody mess right across the street from them. Sitting in the driver seat, he adjusts the rearview mirror and smiles at himself. He tells himself he is free for now.

As he backs out of the driveway and starts his journey home to Louisiana, he cranks up the radio. Despite washing his hands, he catches a slight scent of hot sauce and laughs.

Momma, I'm coming home, blares through the speakers as he smiles to himself and leaves the house he once called home in the rearview mirror.

The End

You made it through one of the most violent books I have ever written. I'm not sure whether that warrants a pat on the back or a call to your nearest therapist but overall, thanks. I appreciate you all reading the disgusting things my brain comes up with, and I will forever be grateful. Now, I know there will be a lot of people that, despite the warning, kept going and read this through to the end, knowing this wasn't their thing. And to those people, I just want to say I made sure to mutilate the guy's dick as well.

Printed in Dunstable, United Kingdom

64586979R00058